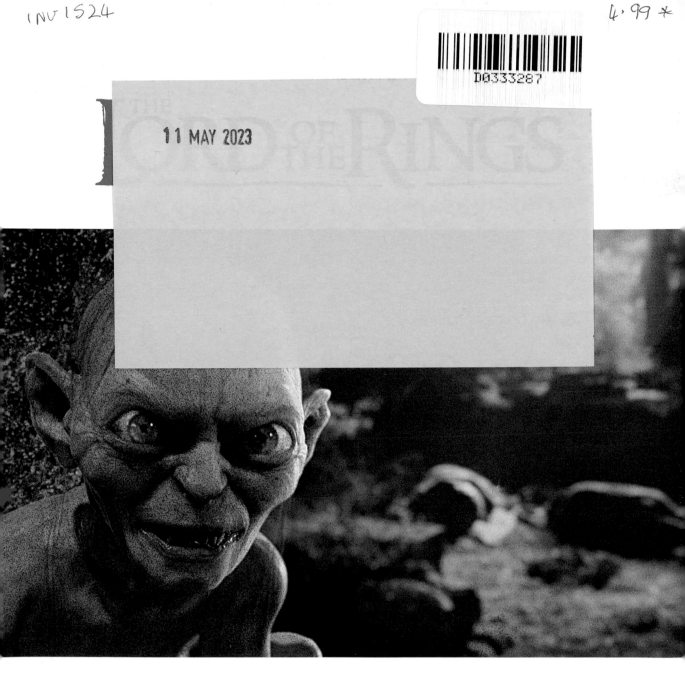

"We shall find it! Yes! We shall find the Precious and keep it for ourselves!"

First published in Great Britain by Collins in 2004

Collins is an imprint of HarperCollinsPublishers
77-85 Fulham Palace Road,
Hammersmith, London W6 8JB

www.tolkien.co.uk

1 3 5 7 9 8 6 4 2

Text by Alison Sage & David Brawn
Adapted from the screenplay by Fran Walsh, Philippa Boyens, Peter Jackson and Stephen Sinclair
Edited by Chris Smith, Design by James Stevens, Production by Ken Clark

Photographs © 2001, 2002, 2003 and 2004 New Line Productions, Inc. All Rights Reserved.
Compilation © HarperCollinsPublishers 2004

The Lord of the Rings, The Fellowship of the Ring, The Two Towers, The Return of the King, and the characters, events,
items and places therein, ™ The Saul Zaentz Company d/b/a Tolkien Enterprises under license to New Line Productions, Inc.
All Rights Reserved.

Tolkien™ is a trademark of The J.R.R. Tolkien Estate Limited.
The Lord of the Rings: Complete Photo Guide is a companion to the films The Fellowship of the Ring, The Two Towers and
The Return of the King and it is published with the permission, but not the approval, of the Estate of the late J.R.R. Tolkien
Dialogue quotations are from the film, not the novel.
The Lord of the Rings and its constituent volumes, The Fellowship of the Ring, The Two Towers and The Return of the King,
are published by HarperCollinsPublishers under licence from The Trustees of The J.R.R. Tolkien 1967 Settlement.

Photographs: Pierre Vinet, with Chris Coad and Ken George
A catalogue record for this book is available from the British Library

ISBN 0 00 719894 9

Printed and bound in Slovenia

THE LORD OF THE RINGS

THE FELLOWSHIP OF THE RING
THE TWO TOWERS
THE RETURN OF THE KING

Trilogy Photo Guide

Collins

An imprint of HarperCollinsPublishers

"One Ring to rule them all,
One Ring to find them,
One Ring to bring them all and
in the darkness bind them
In the Land of Mordor
where the Shadows lie."

THE FELLOWSHIP
OF THE RING

 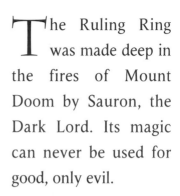

The Ruling Ring was made deep in the fires of Mount Doom by Sauron, the Dark Lord. Its magic can never be used for good, only evil.

"Sauron himself forged the One Ring. The molten gold was mixed with his own blood..."

Sauron loses the Ring in battle but he cannot rest until it is found...

His net spreads wide and he discovers that it is now in the hands of a hobbit called Bilbo Baggins, who lives with his nephew, Frodo, at Bag End in Hobbiton in the Shire.

"Smoke rises once more from the Mountain of Doom: the Shadow takes shape in the darkness of Mordor."

Frodo Baggins: *"Far too eager and curious for a hobbit."*

Few of the peoples of Middle-earth know much about hobbits. They live in holes and mostly keep themselves to themselves. But Frodo and Bilbo are different. They have always taken any chance to visit the world outside the Shire.

"Hobbits really are amazing creatures. You can learn all that there is to know about their ways in a month, and yet, after a hundred years, they can still surprise you…"

*"He's up to something,
I'm sure of it."*

Most hobbits are wary of Bilbo's friend, Gandalf the wizard. He has a strange knack of turning up when something very important is about to happen.

"A wizard is never late, Frodo Baggins, nor is he early. He arrives precisely when he is meant to."

"Half the Shire's been invited and the rest of them are turning up anyway."

The Shire is buzzing with tales of mad Bilbo Baggins and the preparations for his most amazing birthday party.

Little does Frodo suspect that this party is going to change both their lives for ever…

"They are one, the Ring and the Dark Lord. Frodo, he must never find it!"

Gandalf the wizard tells Frodo about the Ring. Bilbo has left the Shire and Frodo is now the new Ring-bearer. But how can one hobbit hope to keep the Ring from all the forces of Sauron?

*"Through me, it would
wield a power too great
and terrible to imagine.
Do not tempt me, Frodo."*

*"The Ring is yours now…
Keep it secret, keep it safe."*

"Mr Frodo's not going anywhere without me!"

Sam is the youngest son of Old Gaffer Gamgee, the gardener at Bag End, and as sensible a young hobbit as any in the Shire. He is fiercely loyal to Frodo.

"If I take one more step, it'll be the farthest from home I've ever been."

"You need people of intelligence for this sort of mission... quest... thing."

"Well, that rules you out, Pip."

Merry (Meriadoc Brandybuck), and Pippin (Peregrin Took) guess that their cousin, Frodo, is planning an adventure and they are determined not to be left behind...

*"It's a dangerous business going
out of your door... You step on to the road and
if you don't keep your feet, there's no knowing
where you might be swept off to."*

The Ring can only be destroyed in the fires of Mount Doom in Mordor. Frodo sets out with Pippin, Merry and Sam on his long mission, knowing that he will be marked by every evil servant of Sauron.

"That Black Rider was looking for something... or someone..."

Gandalf the Grey is a member of the *Istari* – the Order of Wizards – who have been sent to help Middle-earth in their time of need. He is Frodo's friend and guide, although Frodo does not realise quite how powerful he is.

Saruman the White is senior even to Gandalf. He watches the world from the tower of Orthanc. Leaving Frodo behind, Gandalf travels alone to tell Saruman about the Ring, but learns he is not to be trusted.

"The world has changed, Gandalf.
A new Age is at hand…"

"Sauron's only measure is desire for power…
and so he will not think that, having the Ring, we may seek to destroy it."

Having failed to persuade Gandalf to join forces with both himself and the Dark Lord, Sauron, Saruman defeats Gandalf in a battle of magic then imprisons him at the top of Orthanc tower.

"Embrace the power of the Ring...
or embrace your own destruction!"

But when all hope seems lost, Gandalf is rescued by Gwaihir, Lord of Eagles, and flown to safety.

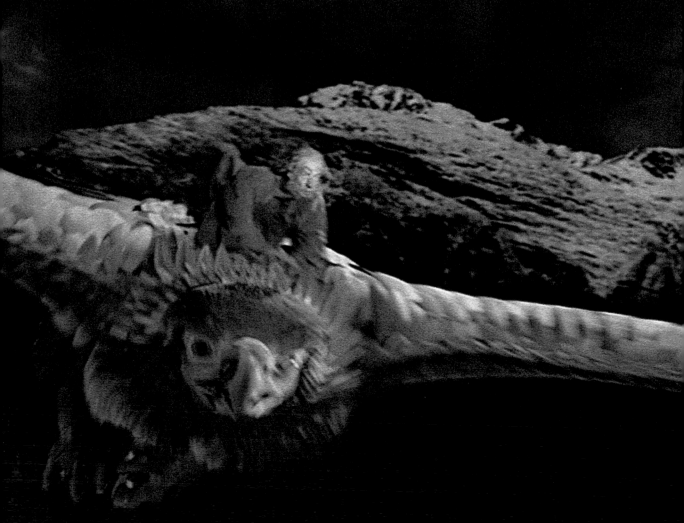

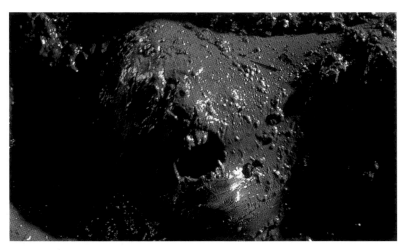

Saruman has his own army, created from some of the most hideous life-forms in Middle-earth.

"By foul craft he has crossed Orcs with goblin men."

"And now… perfected. Grown beyond the height of Men – straight-limbed and strong, fearing nothing."

Leaving the Shire, the hobbits reach The Prancing Pony inn at Bree, hoping to find Gandalf the wizard. Instead, they find a tall, stern man who claims to be their friend. He warns them that they are in desperate danger from the Ringwraiths, the terrible Black Riders of Sauron.

"He's one of them Rangers, dangerous folk they are. Wandering the wilds. What his right name is I've never heard; but he's known round here as Strider."

Strider's true name is Aragorn and he is more than he seems… He is heir to the throne of Gondor.

"You are Isildur's heir, not Isildur himself. You are not bound to his fate."

"I must take you on paths few dare to tread."

"They were Kings... great Kings of Men.
Sauron gave to them Nine Rings of Power.
They took the Rings... and one by one, regardless
of their strength to good or evil... they fell."

Strider leads the hobbits to Weathertop, an isolated hill where they make camp. Here, they are attacked by the Ringwraiths. Sam, Merry and Pippin bravely defend Frodo from their assault but these servants of Sauron are too powerful and soon Frodo faces them alone.

"Back you devils!"

Strider battles the Ringwraiths away with fire, but before he can reach Frodo the terrified hobbit puts on the Ring, and sees the true face of the approaching Witch King, the Ringwraith's leader, who stabs Frodo with his Morgul-knife.

"He's been stabbed by a Morgul blade. This is beyond my skill to heal. He needs Elvish medicine."

Strider tells the hobbits to follow him to Rivendell, the home of Elrond Half-elven. They are in terrible danger, but at their darkest moment the Elven princess Arwen, Elrond's daughter, arrives to rescue them...

"Ride hard –
don't look back."

"The road is too dangerous."

At Rivendell, Elrond calls a council of all the free people of Middle-earth, to decide how to destroy the Ring. Frodo is not to carry the Ring alone. There will be Nine Companions to stand against the Nine Servants of Sauron.

"Rivendell will soon become an island under siege. The Ring cannot stay here."

"The Ring was made in the fires of Mount Doom... Only there can it be unmade."

With his double-headed battle-axe, Gimli is a great Orc-killer and eager to join the Companions.

"Gimli, Glóin's son... known him since he was knee-high to a hobbit."

Legolas has many special powers: his eyesight is sharper than an eagle's and his aim is deadly. Gimli and Legolas are so different, they are bound to clash. But both are united in their desire to see the Ring destroyed.

"Thranduil of the Woodland Realm has sent his son, Legolas."

"The Ring must be destroyed."

"Nine Companions to match the Nine Ringwraiths... So be it."

*"I will take the Ring
to Mordor."*

*"We're coming too! You'll have to send us home tied
up in a sack to stop us!"*

"You have my bow..."

"And my axe."

"If by my life or death, I can protect you, I will. You have my sword."

"I will help you bear this burden, Frodo."

"You carry the fate of us all, little one."

The Fellowship of the Ring

It is time for the Nine Companions to leave Rivendell and set out on their mission.

Bilbo gives Frodo two of his own treasures: his sword, Sting, and a shirt of chainmail made from *mithril*, which is light as a feather and as hard as diamond.

"Sting was made by the Elves. The blade glows blue when Orcs are close."

"May the blessing of Elves and Men and all free folk go with you."

"There is weakness – there is frailty – but there is courage also, and honour, to be found in Men."

Proud and ambitious, Boromir is a man from the ancient Kingdom of Gondor. He carries with him a great horn, tipped with silver, which he has only to blow for help to arrive.

But the test he faces may be too hard, even if the whole of Gondor comes to his rescue.

"Why not use the Ring?"

"It is a strange fate that we suffer so much fear and doubt over so small a thing."

"The road goes ever on and on
Down from the door where it began.
Now far ahead the road has gone
And I must follow, if I can."

Always aware of the danger from the spies of Sauron, the Companions struggle upwards on the treacherous paths through the Misty Mountains. As they continue, snow falls and the road becomes impassable.

"It is not the strength of the body that matters,
but the strength of the spirit."

Gandalf knows of a secret way under the mountains, through the fabled Kingdom of Moria. But how will they find the password to let them through the Gateway?

"Dwarf doors are invisible when closed. Their own masters cannot find them if their secret is forgotten."

"Ithildin – it mirrors only starlight and moonlight."

"Moria – greatest of the Dwarf halls."

"I fear the Dwarves of Moria may have delved too deep."

Almost unimaginable terrors lurk beneath the mountain, and the old Mines of Moria have been overrun by the powers of darkness. The Fellowship must tread quietly if they are to journey through the Dwarven halls without disturbing any enemies.

"Be on your guard... there are older and fouler things than Orcs in the deep places of the world."

"Here lies Balin, son of Fundin, Lord of Moria."

The Orcs hear the noise made by Pippin and thousands of them pour out of their dark caves, screaming as they charge towards the Fellowship.

"They were once elves. Taken by the dark powers,
tortured, mutilated
– a ruined and terrible
form of life, bred into
a slave race."

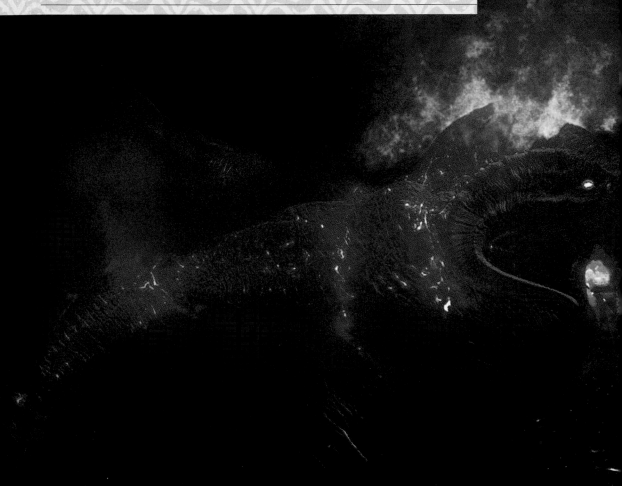

Pursued by Orcs, the Fellowship make for the only exit, reached across a narrow bridge that spans a bottomless chasm. But a terrifying monster rises out of the darkness to stop them: the Balrog, a demon of the ancient world.

Gandalf stands alone on the bridge, and the wizard and the mighty Balrog do battle!

"You shall not pass!"

The Fellowship pay a high price for their escape from Moria. Nine entered the Dwarven kingdom but only eight leave.

"I have heard tell of the strange magic of the Golden Wood..."

The Fellowship stumble on the hidden Elven Kingdom of Lothlórien, the realm of Lord Celeborn and Galadriel, Lady of Light. But the Companions dare not rest for long.

Galadriel takes Frodo to look into her mirror. There he sees fragments from his future…

"Even the smallest person can change the course of the future."

"What you see I cannot tell, for the mirror shows many things… things that were… things that are and some things that have not yet come to pass."

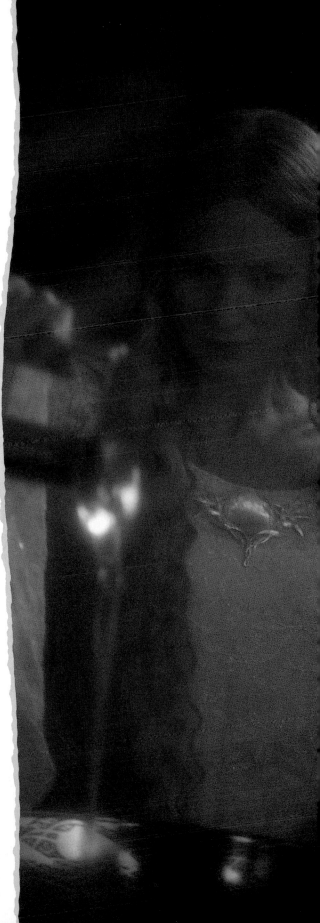

The Fellowship reach Amon Hen, and are attacked by Saruman's Uruk-hai, led by Lurtz. Boromir scares Frodo into running away, but he makes amends by defending Merry and Pippin from the Uruk-hai, killing many.

The numbers are too great, though, and eventually he falls to Lurtz's arrows. Aragorn arrives and slays the Uruk leader, but he is too late to save Boromir. The Fellowship is now broken.

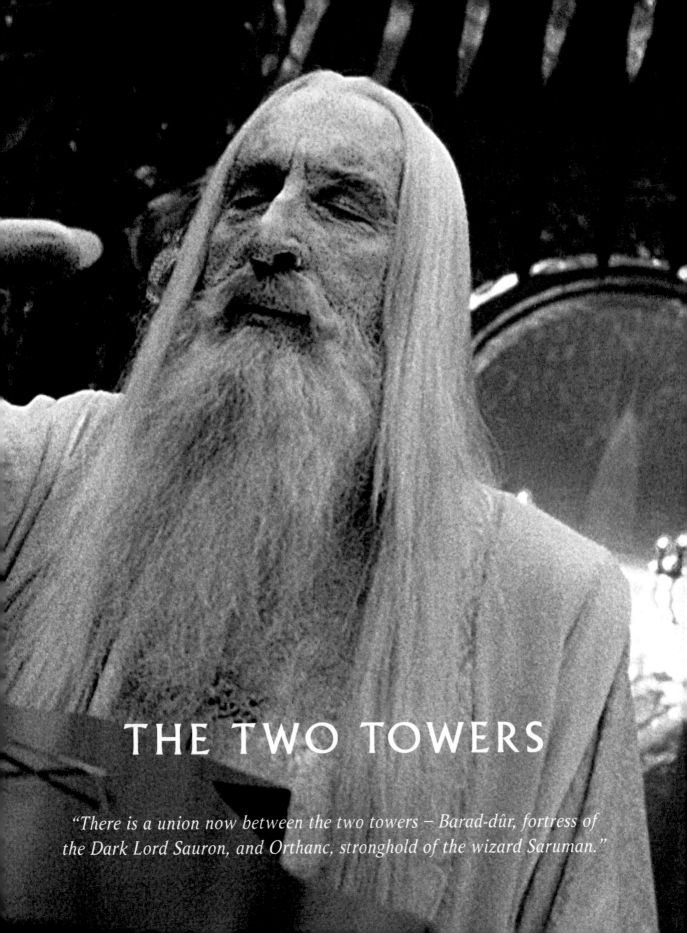

THE TWO TOWERS

"There is a union now between the two towers – Barad-dûr, fortress of the Dark Lord Sauron, and Orthanc, stronghold of the wizard Saruman."

Frodo Baggins is troubled by nightmares. Since undertaking the mission to carry the One Ring back to the place it was made, Mount Doom in Mordor, the hobbit has faced many dangers. His friend Gandalf, the grey wizard, fell to certain death in the Mines of Moria while saving the rest of the Fellowship from the fiery Balrog; and now the traitorous Saruman has sent his army of Uruk-hai after them to retrieve the Ring. No longer knowing who to trust, Frodo breaks from the Fellowship to go on alone – alone, that is, except for his loyal companion, Samwise Gamgee.

"What is it, Mr Frodo?"

"Nothing. A dream."

*"Mordor… the one place in Middle-earth we don't want to see any closer;
and it's the one place we're trying to get to."*

The journey is long and tiring. Sam is worried that they have come the wrong way, and Frodo is frustrated by their lack of speed. To make progress, they know they must get out of the hills and into the wasteland below.

But, someone is following them – someone who is waiting for an opportunity to seize the Ring…

"My preciousss…"

Separated from the others, Merry Brandybuck and Pippin Took are prisoners of Saruman's Uruk-hai warriors, who are now taking them back to their base at Isengard.

"I think we might have made a mistake leaving the Shire, Pippin."

Their captors are debating about why Saruman has ordered them to capture the two young hobbits.

"They have something… some Elvish weapon… the Master wants it for the war."

Pippin tells Merry what he has overheard.

"They think we have the Ring!"

"Shhhh – as soon as they find out we don't, we're dead!"

The three remaining members of the Fellowship of the Ring – Aragorn, Legolas and Gimli – desperately search for their captured friends for three days and nights. They discover Pippin's Elven brooch on the Plains of Rohan.

"They are alive!"

*"Rohan…
home of the horse-lords."*

The arrival of a hundred mighty horsemen, the Riders of Rohan, takes them by surprise. Their leader, Éomer, is Third Marshal of the Riddermark and nephew of King Théoden.

*"What business does
an Elf, a Man,
and a Dwarf have
in the Riddermark?"*

The Uruks' camp is attacked by Éomer's riders, and in the confusion Merry and Pippin escape. Fleeing into Fangorn Forest, the two hobbits are chased by the angry Grishnákh.

"Filthy little squeakers! I'm gonna cut maggot holes in your belly!"

An unexpected ally comes to their rescue.

"What are you?"

"I am an Ent. Treebeard, some call me."

Aragorn, Legolas and Gimli follow the hobbits' trail into the eerie Fangorn Forest. Suddenly, they glimpse an old man watching them through the trees.

"Saruman!"   "The White Wizard…"   "No! It cannot be… Gandalf!"

Standing before them is their friend and guide, Gandalf, restored to life.

"Far beneath the living earth… I fought him – the Balrog of Morgoth. Darkness took me… But it was not the end. The task was not done – I was sent back."

"He is the lord of all horses and has been a friend to me through many dangers."

The renewed Gandalf tells his friends that Merry and Pippin are safe, and that they must leave the forest. War is coming to Rohan and they are needed there. At the edge of the forest Gandalf summons his horse, Shadowfax.

Frodo and Sam finally catch the secretive figure who has been following them. It is Gollum, who once possessed the Ring and was corrupted by its power. He begs to serve Frodo, the *"Master of the Preciousss"*. Frodo accepts on one condition:

"You know the way to Mordor. You've been there before. Take us to the Black Gate."

Gollum leads the hobbits across a gloomy, bleak landscape, full of stagnant pools and withered reeds. But Sam doesn't trust him.

"It's a bog... he's led us into a swamp!"

As they continue their journey across the Marshes, Gollum tells them how his cousin, Déagol, found the Ring many years ago while they were out fishing. Gollum, or Sméagol as he was known then, wanted the Ring so much that he killed his cousin and stole it.

"Murderer they called us… and sent us away."

After committing this terrible crime, Gollum fled from his home and went to live in a cave under the Misty Mountains with only the Ring for company. There he grew wretched and miserable and full of self pity.

Reunited once more, Gandalf and his three companions gallop towards Edoras, the capital of Rohan.

"Meduseld, the Court of Edoras, where dwells Théoden, King of Rohan."

Approaching the Golden Hall, their way is blocked by the King's Guard.

"I cannot let you before the king so armed, Gandalf Greyhame, by order of Gríma Wormtongue."

"Would you part an old man from his walking stick?"

The king's niece, Éowyn, is mourning the death of her cousin, Théodred, who was fatally injured in battle against Saruman's Orcs. Now she grows worried for the safety of her brother, Éomer.

Éowyn is pestered by the king's counsellor, the loathsome Gríma Wormtongue, who is captivated by her even though she despises him.

"Leave me alone, snake... Your words are poison."

"I understand. His passing is hard to accept – especially now that your brother has deserted you."

"Ever have you been the herald of woe. Why should I welcome you, Gandalf Stormcrow?"

Gandalf is taken before King Théoden and is shocked at how old the monarch has grown since they last met. He senses Saruman's influence over the king…

"Too long have you sat in the shadows. Harken to me! I release you from this spell!"

Gríma Wormtongue realises what is happening but reacts too late.

*"His staff!
I told you to take
the wizard's staff!"*

Released from Saruman's power, Théoden comes to his senses, regaining his old strength. Wormtongue is revealed to be a traitor, and the king throws him out of the palace.

"Ever his whispering was in your ears... poisoning your thoughts."

"Banishment is too good for you."

Saruman is furious that Gandalf has released King Théoden from his spell. Now more drastic actions are required to conquer the kingdom of Rohan.

Arming a rabble of five hundred Dunlendings and Wild Men, savages who live in the hills around Rohan, Saruman sends them on a rampage of chaos and destruction.

"Take back the lands they stole from you. Burn every village!"

"This is but a taste of the terror Saruman will unleash..."

Gandalf counsels King Théoden to send his troops to fight Saruman's army and draw them away from the women and children. The king decides to evacuate the city and take all his people to the safety of the mighty fortress of Helm's Deep.

Aragorn helps to oversee the departure of the last of the horses. Brego, the battle-worn steed of the dead prince, Théodred, is too distressed to carry another rider.

"Turn this fellow free. He has seen enough of war."

Gollum leads Frodo and Sam to the Black Gates of Mordor which span a deep valley between the grim, grey mountains. They are guarded by fierce Orc sentries.

"Master says bring usss to the Gatesss, so good Sméagol does."

A long column of fearsome-looking Easterlings march past Sam and Frodo and through the great iron gates into Mordor.

"Well that's it, then. We can't get in there."

Gríma Wormtongue returns to his true master. He tells Saruman that King Théoden's instinct will be to make for Helm's Deep. Saruman decides to send his Orcs to attack the refugees.

"Théoden made two mistakes.
First he trusted you, then he let you live."

At the City of the Trees, Elrond calls a council of the Elves. He believes that they should help in the struggle against Sauron, but not everyone agrees.

"The Rings of the Elf Lords were not made as weapons of war or conquest. They cannot come to the aid of Men."

"The alliance between Men and Elves is over."

Later, Elrond confronts his daughter Arwen about her decision to stay behind with Aragorn. By pledging her love to a mortal man, she must accept that she will grow old and die with him while her people remain young for ever. Elrond thinks she has made the wrong choice.

"There is nothing here for you, only death."

As the refugees and soldiers pass through the mountains, they are ambushed by Orcs riding giant wolf-beasts. They break ranks to engage the legion of snarling Wargs which attack them, and Aragorn becomes locked in a deadly battle with Sharku.

Reaching the woods of Ithilien, Frodo and Sam run into a party of Gondorian Rangers, who mistake them for Orc spies. They are blindfolded and taken to their hideaway, Henneth Annûn.

The Rangers discover the nature of Frodo's mission. Hearing that Boromir was one of the Fellowship, the Rangers' leader, Faramir, has shocking news…

"You were a friend of Boromir?
It would grieve you, then, to learn that he is dead?"

Faramir reveals that he is Boromir's brother and the son of Lord Denethor, the Steward of Gondor. Learning of the One Ring, he vows to take the Ring to Gondor, and complete Boromir's mission.

Treebeard carries Merry and Pippin deep into the forest. They reach the Entmoot, a gathering of many different tree-people, and wait patiently while the spirits of the forest discuss their fate.

"It's been going on for hours."

"They must have decided something by now."

"Decided? We've only just finished saying Good Morning!"

Merry and Pippin's appeal to the Ents to help in the fight against the evil of Isengard stirs them up, and they agree to march to Saruman's lair.

"It is likely, my friends, that we go to our doom: the last march of the Ents..."

The refugees and Rohan soldiers finally reach the ancient fortress of Helm's Deep. They gather in the Hornburg courtyard.

As Legolas and Gimli gallop through the gates, King Théoden tells Éowyn how they were ambushed and that many of their number were killed.

"Lord Aragorn – where is he?"

"He fell defending the retreat."

Having fallen in battle with Sharku, Aragorn is barely alive. As he struggles to get up, an unexpected champion comes to his aid.

"Brego...?"

Brought safely to Helm's Deep by Brego, Aragorn has urgent news for King Théoden. He has seen thousands of Uruk-hai marching towards the fortress.

"All Isengard has emptied... Ten thousand strong at least. It is an army bred for one purpose – to destroy the world of Men."

Legolas is worried: the defenders are frightened, and he fears three hundred of them cannot hold out against an army of ten thousand Uruk-hai. He feels betrayed by his own people and believes that the Elves should not have left the Men to stand alone.

The Uruks reach Helm's Deep and the great battle begins!

The Rangers reach Osgiliath, once one of the greatest cities in all of Gondor, but now in ruins after years of war. Faramir intends to take Frodo with him to the city of Minas Tirith and use the Ring in their struggle against Sauron. Sam pleads with him:

"The Ring will not save Gondor."

Faramir finally sees the evil in the Ring and realises that it is impossible to use it for good. He is persuaded to let Frodo, Sam and Gollum continue their journey to Mordor, and leads them to the old sewers where they can pass underneath the patrolling Orcs.

"Go, Frodo, go with the good will of all Men."

Merry and Pippin arrive at Isengard with the marching Ents. From his tower, Saruman watches as the massive tree-people break down the walls around his stronghold.

"There is a wizard to manage here… locked in his tower!"

Meanwhile, weary from the battle of Helm's Deep, Gandalf the White warns his friends that they have not seen the last of the Orcs and their kind.

"*Sauron's wrath will be terrible and his retribution swift. The battle for Helm's Deep is over. The battle for Middle-earth is about to begin.*"

THE RETURN OF THE KING

*"All our hopes now lie with two little hobbits…
somewhere in the wilderness."*

Sauron's plans for the conquest of Middle-earth are nearing completion. He is drawing together an army from regions throughout the land, including the fearsome Haradrim, Easterlings, Orcs and Trolls.

His nine Ringwraiths patrol the skies on wicked Fell Beasts, and his anger is growing. For the most unlikely of heroes are struggling to prevent Sauron's domination:

The Ents, ancient and normally peaceful tree-folk, have destroyed the fortress of his great ally, Saruman;

The rural-dwelling Riders of Rohan have defeated an army of specially bred Uruk-hai warriors at Helm's Deep;

And Gollum, a twisted halfling sent by Sauron to retrieve the One Ring, has disappeared from sight.

The ancient wizard Gandalf, thought killed in the Mines of Moria, is conspiring with the heir of Elendil to unite all the Free Peoples against the Dark Lord.

"If the Ring is destroyed, then Sauron will fall, and his fall will be so low that none will see his arising ever again. But if Sauron regains the Ring, his victory will be swift and complete."

As his daughter Arwen lies dying, Lord Elrond of the Elves arranges for the ancient shards of Narsil, the blade that cut down Sauron centuries ago, to be reforged into a new and mighty sword, a weapon so powerful that even the Dead begin to stir…

Pippin Took cannot sleep. The destruction of Isengard is playing on his mind, and he has become fascinated by Saruman's seeing stone, brought back by Gandalf from the Tower of Orthanc.

"What are you doing?"

"I just wanted to look at it…"

"Pippin – no!"

Aragorn snatches the palan-tír away. But it is too late – Gandalf realises the hobbit is now in great danger.

"Things are now in motion that cannot be undone. Sauron has looked into the face of young Peregrin Took and mistaken him for the Ring-bearer."

Gandalf decides he must take Pippin to safety. As they ride out on Shadowfax, Pippin's friend Merry asks where they are going.

"To the safest place in Middle-earth… the city of Minas Tirith."

Frodo Baggins, weighed down by the burden of carrying the One Ring to Mordor, now has two companions to encourage him: his faithful servant Sam Gamgee, and their new guide Gollum.

"Come on, we must go, no time, no time to lose."

They reach a crossroads where the ancient statue of a Gondorian king sits, still and solemn. Orcs have toppled the statue's head and replaced it with a crude carving. Frodo is saddened by it.

"These lands were once part of the Kingdom of Gondor… long ago when there was a king and the West stood strong."

As they continue on, Sam overhears Gollum talking to himself.

"Let her deal with them. She must eat… the Precious will be ours once the hobbitses are dead!"

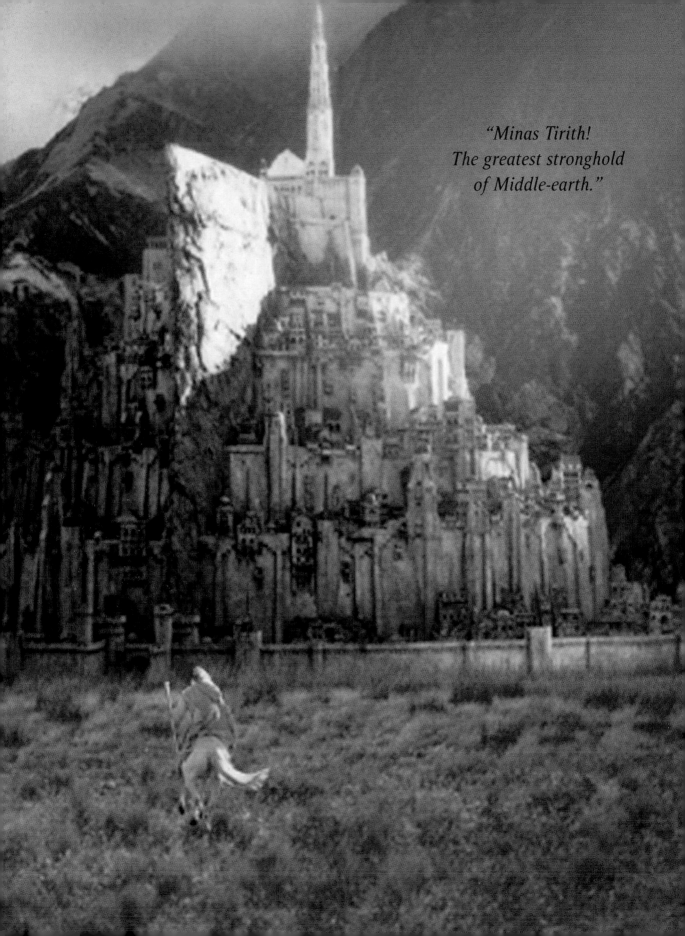

*"Minas Tirith!
The greatest stronghold
of Middle-earth."*

Entering the White City, Gandalf and Pippin ride up hundreds of steps to the seventh level, the Court of the Kings, a thousand feet above the ground.

"Gandalf, why are they guarding a dead tree?"

Gandalf explains how the White Tree has withered as the rule of Gondor has waned. The citadel guards protect the tree in the belief that it, like Gondor, might one day flourish once more.

In the throne room, Gandalf meets Denethor, the Ruling Steward of Gondor. He is a gloomy and bitter old man, who is angry about the death of his son Boromir, and he warns Gandalf that Aragorn will not be welcome here.

"The rule of Gondor is mine, and no other's!"

"Authority is not given to you, Steward Gondor, to deny the return of the King."

When Gandalf has gone, Denethor is reunited with his second son, Faramir. He is furious that Faramir has allowed Frodo to take the Ring of Power into Mordor when he could have brought it back here. He reminds himself of the two brothers before they left.

"Boromir would have remembered his father's need. He would have brought me a kingly gift!"

Pippin is on a mission for Gandalf. Creeping on to the battlements, he lights the massive beacon on top of the city. It is a signal to others that war has begun.

Across the plains at Edoras, Aragorn bursts into the Golden Hall.

"The beacons of Minas Tirith! Gondor calls for aid!"

As King Théoden rallies the Riders of Rohan, he receives an unexpected offer.

*"I have a sword.
I offer you my service,
Théoden King."*

*"Gladly I receive it –
you shall be Meriadoc,
Esquire of Rohan,
and ride with me."*

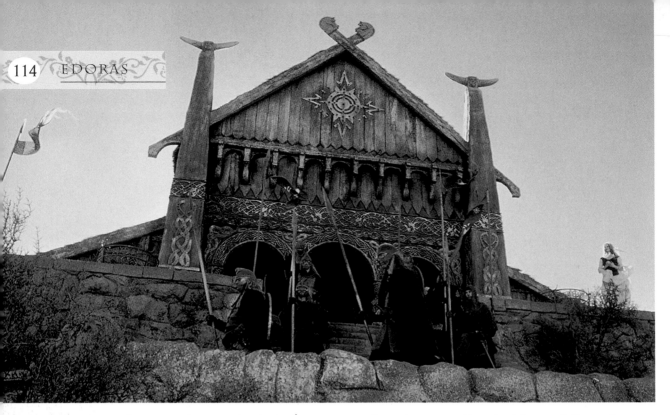

As the Rohirrim ride out, the lady Éowyn watches them go. She decides to follow them…

Pippin has joined the Tower Guard. He has been given the only hobbit-sized uniform they have – it was made for Faramir when he was just a boy.

Meanwhile, Faramir leads 200 knights out of the city to go and confront the evil forces that have invaded the neighbouring city of Osgiliath.

Night has fallen and the Riders of Rohan have set up camp at Dunharrow. Aragorn is summoned to meet an unexpected guest in King Théoden's tent. Elrond has a gift for Aragorn.

"Andúril, flame of the West… forged from the shards of Narsil. The man whocan wield the power of this sword can summon to him an army more deadly than any that walk this earth!"

Aragorn realises what he must do – go to summon the Oath-breakers who dwell in the haunted mountain, from where none have ever returned.

"Every path you have trod, through wilderness, through war, has led to this road. This is your test, Aragorn."

Gimli and Legolas insist on accompanying their friend on his new quest.

"We're going to follow you, lad – even on the dark Road..."
"...To wherever it may lead."

The next day, the entire camp is on the move – they ride to war. Merry is preparing to go with them, but King Théoden has other ideas.

"Little hobbits do not belong in war, Master Meriadoc."

"I want to fight!"

Then, as all hope seems lost, a young rider pulls Merry up on to a horse.

Faramir's horse has returned to Minas Tirith, dragging its badly wounded master behind it. His men were ambushed by the Orcs at Osgiliath.

"They were outnumbered, none survived."

Denethor is heartbroken – he believes both his sons are now dead.

"The House of Stewards has failed! My line has ended."

*"The living are not welcome
on this road."*

Aragorn, Legolas and Gimli make
their way up a gloomy canyon to
the Dwimorberg Mountain. It is a
desolate and eerie place.

*"Long ago the men of the
mountain swore an oath to
the last King of Gondor to
come to his aid…
Isildur cursed them never
to rest until they fulfilled
their pledge."*

"Who enters my domain?"

In the dark passages under the mountain, ghoulish hands reach up out of the mist, and a mummified spectre looms out of the fog ahead of them. It is the King of the Dead.

"None but the King of Gondor may command me!"

Raising his sacred sword in answer, Aragorn addresses the ghost army.

"Fight and regain your honour. Fight and I will release you from this living death!"

Minas Tirith is under attack. The vast Orc army has advanced from Osgiliath, and great siege towers and mighty wooden catapults now surround the city. With the lower level already in flames, the huge gate is smashed open.

Arriving outside the city, King Théoden orders his men to join the battle.

"Fear no darkness! Ride now, ride to ruin and the world's ending!"

On the battlements, the soldiers of Gondor watch in awe as the charge of the Rohirrim closes in on the Orc army.

High above the fighting, Denethor leads a procession carrying Faramir's unconscious body. He has planned a noble death for him and his son.

"No tomb for Denethor and Faramir... we will burn like the heathen kings of old!"

Pippin realises in horror that the Steward of Gondor is quite mad!

"Denethor has lost his mind. He's burning Faramir alive!"

Down on the battlefield, the arrival of the Mûmakil, massive elephant-like creatures carrying war-towers filled with Haradrim bowmen, terrify the horses.

Sensing victory, the evil Witch King joins the battle, to be confronted by Éowyn.

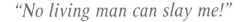

"No living man can slay me!"

"I am no man! You look upon a woman!"

As the Witch King attacks, Merry strikes him from behind, and together they bring him down.

Frodo, Sam and Gollum have reached the pass of Cirith Ungol on their way to Mount Doom. Thousands of armour-clad Orcs have passed them, marching to war.

"The board is set, the pieces are moving.
We come to it at last ... the great battle of our time."

Persuaded by Gollum to leave Sam behind, Frodo advances into the pass of Cirith Ungol, a dark tunnel through the mountains. It is filled with rotting things and the odour of unspeakable decay, and as they move forward, Frodo hears a gurgling, venomous hiss from the shadows.

"What was that? Sméagol?"

But Gollum has deserted him!

In the darkness, Frodo remembers Galadriel's gift – the star-glass of Eärendil. He pulls it from his jacket, but the light it casts reveals a nightmare... Shelob, a huge and loathsome Spider!

Shagrat and Gorbag – an
Uruk and an Orc – come to
Shelob's lair to scavenge for
her spoils. They find Frodo's
lifeless body.

*"Looks like old Shelob's
been having some fun!"*

*"The little filth'll
wake up in a
few hours…"*

*"…And then he'll wish
he'd never
been born!"*

In the dark Orc watch-tower at Cirith Ungol, Frodo wakes to find himself a prisoner.

He freezes, as Gorbag climbs into the room.

"I'm gonna bleed you like a stuck pig!"

Just then, a rescuer appears out of the shadows.

"Sam!!!"

The defenders of Minas Tirith are horrified to see the black ships of the Corsairs of Umbar sailing up the River Anduin. Sauron's Orcs expect to welcome pirate reinforcements, but instead they are greeted by Aragorn, Legolas and Gimli followed by 5,000 soldiers of the Army of the Dead, who sweep through Sauron's army. Those Orcs and mûmakil who are not killed flee in terror.

"For Middle-earth!"

Disguising themselves as Orcs, Frodo and Sam leave the tower and set out for Mount Doom. They have entered Sauron's realm of Mordor, and are at last within sight of their goal!

The battlefield has fallen silent. Sauron's army has been defeated, but it is a scene of devastation, where the bodies outnumber the living.

Pippin is relieved to find Merry is only wounded.

"Come on Merry, up you get,
we must get you to the city..."

At Minas Tirith, Faramir lies dying. Helping the elderly nurse Ioreth, Aragorn administers an ancient remedy to his fallen comrade.

"It is said in old lore that the hands of a king are the hands of a healer..."

Arwen is gravely ill. She senses that Sauron is about to regain the Ring, and that the world of Men is almost at an end. With Sauron's death all that will save her, she tells Elrond of her love for Aragorn.

"I wish I could have seen him one last time."

"I'll be an Orc no more, and I will bear no weapon, fair or foul."

Reaching Mount Doom, Frodo and Sam discard their Orc clothing and struggle against the heat and ash as they approach the Crack of Doom. Frodo is exhausted, and Sam offers him the last of their water

"There will be none left for the return journey."

"I don't think there will be a return journey, Mr Frodo."

Knowing that Frodo must be near his goal, and therefore in great danger, Aragorn decides to lead a force of Men to the Black Gates of Mordor. He hopes to distract Sauron and his remaining forces long enough for Frodo to destroy the Ring and break Sauron's power forever.

Riding out, Aragorn, clad in the armour of his forebears, knows he carries the hopes for the future of Middle-earth with him.

"There may come a day when the courage of Men fails; when we forsake our friends and break all bonds of fellowship; an hour of wolves before the Age of Men come crashing down – but it will not be this day! This day we fight!"

Sam and Frodo reach the stone doorway of Sammath Naur, the way into the mountain where the Ring was made. As they stagger inside, the fierce heat is overwhelming.

They do not notice the presence of a familiar figure who has been waiting for them…

"My Precious! My Preciousss!"

Suddenly Gollum appears and tries to claim the Ring for himself. But he is too late!

The One Ring has been destroyed, but Frodo and Sam are trapped on Mount Doom, with fiery lava flowing all around them. Just when it seems like the end for the two heroic hobbits, Gandalf arrives on Gwaihir, Lord of Eagles, and flies them to safety.

"I'm glad to be with you, Samwise Gamgee, here at the end of all things."

Frodo wakes up to find himself in the Houses of Healing. All his friends are together again, and he knows he can finally return home to the Shire.

With Sauron defeated, the days of the King have begun again. At a rich and colourful coronation, Aragorn is crowned King, Arwen is his queen, and the White Tree of Gondor is in full flower again.

*"And thus it was that a Fourth Age of Middle-earth began,
and the Fellowship of the Ring, though eternally bound
by friendship and love, was ended."*

The four hobbits return to the Shire, but the journey is not yet over. They accompany Bilbo to the Grey Havens, where he joins Gandalf, Elrond, Galadriel and Celeborn who are leaving Middle-earth for ever.

"Now here is a sight I have never seen before."

Then, to the hobbits' surprise, Frodo says goodbye to Sam, Merry and Pippin and takes his place aboard the Elven ship, sailing on his final Journey into the sunset.

"I think I'm quite ready for another adventure."

"Still round the corner there may wait
A new road or a secret gate;
And though I oft have passed them by,
A day will come when I
Shall take the hidden paths that run
West of the Moon, East of the Sun."